THIS **BEN 10 OMNIVERSE** ANNUAL BELONGS TO

NAME ....Benjamin gilroy.............................

HOME PLANET ....Earthecrotel.........................

SPECIES ....humansid......................................

SPECIAL ALIEN POWERS ....~~steath~~ ~~travat~~ invisabilaty ~~Mode~~............

EGMONT
We bring stories to life

First published in Great Britain 2013 by Egmont UK Limited
The Yellow Building, 1 Nicholas Road, London W11 4AN

Written by Stephanie Milton. Designed by Ant Duke.

ISBN 978 1 4052 6760 1
54722/1
Printed in Italy

Stay safe online. Any website addresses listed in this book are correct at the time of going to print. However, Egmont is not responsible for content hosted by third parties. Please be aware that online content can be subject to change and websites can contain content that is unsuitable for children. We advise that all children are supervised when using the internet.

CONTENTS

A CHANCE TO WIN £150 OF BOOK TOKENS!
See page 67 for details.

NATIONAL BOOK tokens

A NEW BEGINNING

Ben Tennyson is back! His cousin Gwen left town for college, taking her boyfriend Kevin with her, which means Ben has to save the universe alone from now on. Or so he thinks ...

Grandpa Max has found Ben a new Plumber partner – Rook Blonko. Rook doesn't have any field experience, so it's up to Ben to teach him what it's really like to battle evil aliens.

As well as running into a few old enemies, Ben's being hunted by a mysterious new villain with a powerful weapon. And Ben's about to uncover his hometown's biggest alien secret ...

JOIN BEN AS HE STARTS A NEW CHAPTER OF HIS LIFE, AND GET READY TO GO OMNIVERSE!

BEN TENNYSON

Sixteen-year-old Ben is sad to see Gwen and Kevin leave Bellwood, but he's confident he can save the universe without them. So when Grandpa Max introduces him to his new partner, Rook Blonko, Ben is pretty unimpressed. But once he's seen Rook in action a few times he realises he could be a useful partner, and an all-round cool guy, too. And Ben is really glad to have Rook by his side when he finds himself up against Khyber the Huntsman and his dog!

STRENGTHS: Brave, always ready to help those in trouble.

WEAKNESSES: Doesn't want to accept help from others – can be too confident in his own abilities.

EQUIPMENT: A brand-new Omnitrix with ten new alien heroes to help him save the universe!

HERO

THE OMNITRIX

Ben's new Omnitrix has been updated to include ten brand-new aliens. Unfortunately it doesn't always turn Ben into the alien he needs, and often powers down at the worst possible moment – usually when Ben is right in the middle of fighting the bad guys! The Omnitrix is of great interest to Ben's enemies, many of whom attempt to take it from him. So far Ben's managed to hang on to it …

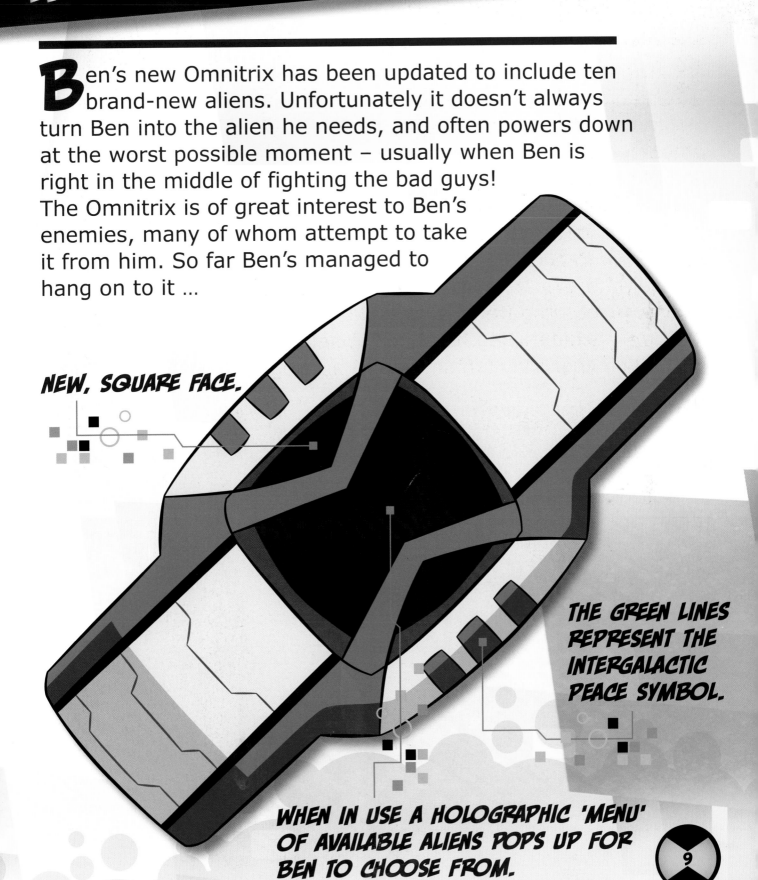

NEW, SQUARE FACE.

THE GREEN LINES REPRESENT THE INTERGALACTIC PEACE SYMBOL.

WHEN IN USE A HOLOGRAPHIC 'MENU' OF AVAILABLE ALIENS POPS UP FOR BEN TO CHOOSE FROM.

9

ROOK BLONKO

When Gwen and Kevin leave town, Grandpa Max finds Ben a new partner – Rook Blonko. Rook is a newly-qualified alien Plumber with a whole lotta training but no field experience. Rook learned all about Ben at the Plumbers' Academy, but Ben finds he can learn a thing or two from Rook as well.

HOME PLANET: Revonnah

SPECIES: Revonnahgander

EQUIPMENT:
- **Proto-Tool – a clever weapon that can transform into whatever Rook needs it to be.**
- **Proto-Tech Armour – very strong to protect him from attack.**
- **Spacecraft – disguises itself as a plumber's van when not in use.**

STRENGTHS:
- **Logical and intelligent.**
- **Acrobatic fighting style.**

HERO

10

UNDERTOWN

Ben's just discovered his hometown's biggest secret: there's a hidden alien city called Undertown built right underneath Bellwood! It's been there for quite some time, but Ben and Rook only discover it whilst chasing down a pack of alien thugs who wreck Baumann's store. They're amazed to see all kinds of aliens living in Undertown as well as everything from bars and a marketplace to its very own transport system.

Sixteen-year-old Ben Tennyson had been abandoned! His cousin Gwen had left Bellwood for college, and she'd taken her boyfriend Kevin with her. The three of them had been saving the universe from alien lowlifes for years – they'd been the perfect team. Ben felt sad, but he knew he'd be able to save the universe alone. He was the famous Ben Tennyson, after all!

Ben headed over to the Plumbers' secret HQ below his Grandpa Max's plumbing shop. He'd barely finished saying hello to Grandpa Max when an explosion from outside shook the base. Ben headed out to investigate, ignoring Grandpa Max's offer of backup. "I don't need backup!" Ben assured him.

Outside, an enormous crater was all that remained of the building next door. Suddenly a huge, snarling beast burst out of the ruins and charged at Ben. He hit his Omnitrix, hoping for Humungousaur, but transformed into Spidermonkey instead. The beast hit Spidermonkey and pinned him to a wall of rubble under his crushing weight. Spidermonkey was powerless!

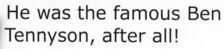

Things were beginning to look bad for Spidermonkey when the beast suddenly whipped its head round, as if it had heard a noise, released Ben and ran off.

"That's right! Keep running!" Spidermonkey yelled as he recovered his breath.

Spidermonkey transformed back into Ben and spotted Pakmar, a tiny alien who ran a toilet emporium in Bellwood. Pakmar told Ben that peace-loving aliens like himself were being forced to pay a pack of low-life alien thugs Taydenite – the most precious gem in the galaxy. If they refused to pay up, the thugs would attack them and destroy their homes and businesses.

Ben needed more information. He marched over to Baumann's alien grocery store and demanded to be told everything that Mr Baumann knew. Baumann admitted that the thugs were on their way over to his store right now. He tried to hurry Ben away, convinced he would only cause more trouble. But Ben didn't listen – he hit the Omnitrix and transformed into Cannonbolt, making a huge racket and drawing the attention of every eye in the shop.

Cannonbolt sat down at the food counter next to a mysterious cloaked alien who was eating with his head down. A moment later the thugs entered the store. They were carrying a strange machine.

"Pay up, Baumann," an alien in a helmet growled, gesturing towards the machine – it was obviously a weapon of some kind. Baumann looked nervously at the machine, grabbed a small box from behind the counter, took out one piece of Taydenite and held it out for the alien. The alien took the whole box instead.

"Hey, Bubble Helmet!" Cannonbolt shouted as the thugs made to leave. Bubble Helmet and the other aliens turned to surround Cannonbolt.

Cannonbolt rolled up into a ball and launched himself at Bubble Helmet, knocking him into a shelf. The shelf started a domino effect, knocking one shelf over after another, until half of Baumann's store was demolished. While Cannonbolt was distracted, Bubble Helmet switched on the machine.

"Let's craterize this place!" he shouted menacingly. A force field flashed around the machine and a countdown clock appeared on the side – it was going to blow!

Cannonbolt smashed into the force field, but he didn't even leave a dent, and the Omnitrix timed out! The thugs started to make their escape.

"Isn't this where your friends show up and save the day?" Baumann called.

As if on cue, the cloaked alien at the counter sprang up. His cloak fell to the floor, revealing black and blue armour and an impressive-looking weapon. The alien jumped into the middle of the bad guys and busted out some awesome moves to take them down. Ben was shocked – this guy was good!

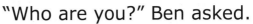

"Who are you?" Ben asked.
"Rook Blonko. Magister Tennyson sent me," the alien replied.
"Grandpa?" Ben was confused.
"I'm your new partner."

"I don't want a new partner!" Ben exclaimed. "No offence, but I'm Ben Tennyson."

"I know. It's an honour to be working with you, sir."

Ben pointed at his wrist. "Wielder of the Omnitrix! I've saved the universe, like, a billion times."

"I am well aware. It's required study at the Plumbers' Academy."

Ben was pleased. "There's a whole class about me?"

"Chapter and a half."

"Oh. Well, I was kind of looking forward to being on my own now. You understand, right? I have things under control here," Ben finished, gesturing vaguely at the demolished store.

Rook surveyed what was left of the shop, then looked at Baumann who was cowering behind the counter, shaking his head.

Two of the thugs rushed past them, trying to flee the scene while Ben and Rook were distracted.

"Don't stop NOW!" Ben snapped. "The Omnitrix is timed out!"

Rook sprang back into action, firing an energy net at the thugs and pinning them to the ground.

Ben was irritated. This guy was beginning to make him look bad. "I bet anybody could do that, if they had one of those ... things," he huffed.

"It's called a Proto-Tool. I've made some special modifications myself," Rook told him. With a flash and a beep the Omnitrix powered back into life. Ben grinned – perfect timing.

"Thanks for the help, man, but I've got this now," Ben said as he hit the Omnitrix and transformed into Bloxx – an alien he'd never seen before. Bloxx took a swing at the force field. His fist shattered, but immediately rebuilt itself. Rook was fighting the thugs again.

"Get over here and disable the force field for me. I'll deal with those guys!" Bloxx shouted.

Bloxx and Rook switched places and Bloxx built himself into a wall to surround the thugs.

But there was less than a minute left on the countdown! Rook blasted through the outer wall of Baumann's shop with his Proto-Tool.

"Help me move it outside!" Rook called to Ben.

Bloxx scooped up the machine and crashed through the wall. Rook scanned the outside area for signs of life, and when they were sure it was clear Bloxx hurled the machine into the abandoned building next door.

The machine exploded, destroying the entire building. Bloxx changed back into Ben, and asked Rook if he was OK. Rook tapped his armour. "Proto-Tech Armour. Nice of you to try to save me though. Thanks, Partner."

"Don't mention it," Ben replied.

Rook looked confused. "But I just did."

"And we're not partners. I work alone now."

"Yes, Sir."

"Call me Ben, dude."

"OK, Ben Dude."

The thugs disappeared into the crater and Ben and Rook took off after them. They soon found themselves in an underground tunnel that opened up to reveal an alien city, built right beneath Bellwood!

"No way …" Ben gasped. How long had this been here? But there was no time to stand around and wonder. He took off after Rook to track down the thugs.

Ben and Rook had no idea that Khyber the Huntsman and his dog had been watching the action outside. Khyber led his dog down into the crater. "Show no mercy," he commanded as his dog transformed into a snarling, alien beast and set off to hunt Ben down.

CONTINUED ON PAGE 29

ODD OMNITRIX OUT

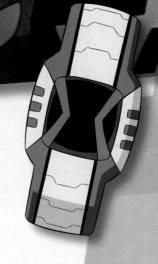

Only one of these pictures is the real Omnitrix. Can you find it using the picture at the top as a guide?

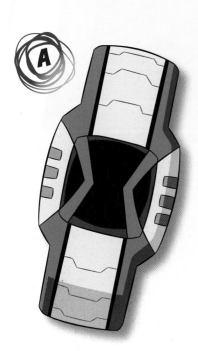

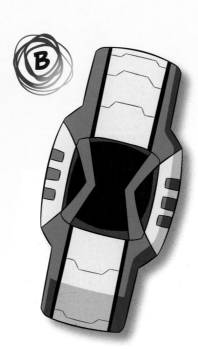

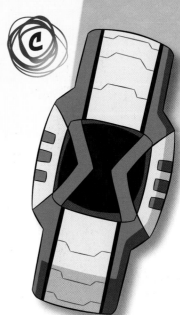

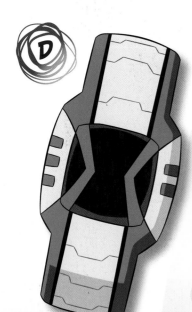

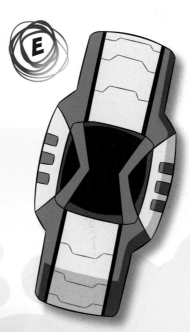

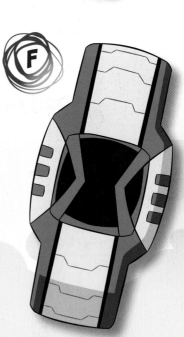

UNDERTOWN SHOWDOWN

Ben and Rook are chasing some alien thugs through Undertown. Can you help them catch up by choosing the right path through the maze? Make sure you don't run into Crabdozer along the way!

Start

Finish

Ten-year-old Ben Tennyson was just an ordinary boy looking forward to the summer holidays, until a family camping trip with Grandpa Max and his cousin Gwen changed his life forever. While Ben was taking a walk in the forest, a meteor fell to earth and almost squished him. Except it wasn't a meteor – it was a strange watch-like device that attached itself to Ben's wrist and refused to come off! Ben soon realised it was more than just a watch when he transformed into the alien Heatblast. He accidentally started a forest fire, which wasn't cool, but then he turned into Diamondhead to fight off an alien attack, which was very, VERY cool!

STRENGTHS: Loyal and fearless.

WEAKNESSES: Often rushes into things without thinking, a bit of a show-off.

EQUIPMENT: The original Omnitrix.

HERO

PROFILE:

FEEDBACK

Exclusive to young Ben, Feedback is an alien powerhouse who can absorb energy then blast it at his enemies through his long, cable-like tentacles. He can also use his tentacles to drain energy from his opponents.

HOME PLANET: Teslavorr

SPECIES: Conductoid

STRENGTHS: Can absorb energy and then shoot it at his enemies.

HERO

PROFILE:
SHOCKSQUATCH

Shocksquatch is a large, yellow alien who looks like a yeti. He has super strength and the power to control electricity. He can charge himself up and fire bolts at his opponents, which is why his fur looks like it's standing on end!

HOME PLANET: Pattersonea

SPECIES: Gimlinopithecus

STRENGTHS: Can shock his opponents. Super strength.

HERO

BLOXX

Bloxx is a shape-shifting alien made up of lots of coloured blocks. He can transform into a variety of different forms to dodge his enemies, protect himself or rebuild himself when he gets injured. He can also transform into different containers when he needs to restrain his enemies or pick things up.

HERO

HOME PLANET: Polyominus

SPECIES: Segmentasapien

STRENGTHS: Can shape-shift into different forms and rebuild himself if he gets injured.

LOOK AGAIN

Something funny is going on in Undertown. Can you spot 10 differences between these two pictures?

ALIEN SWARM

How many aliens can you count on this page? Write your answer below.

THERE ARE ....ALIENS.

CRASHHOPPER

Crashhopper is an insect-like alien with powerful legs which help him jump long distances. Being able to jump like a rocket helps him ram into his opponents with a lot of force. Sometimes he lands so hard that he makes a crater and destroys whatever it is he landed on.

HERO

HOME PLANET: Unknown

SPECIES: Unknown

STRENGTHS: Can jump long distances.

27

PROFILE:
GRAVATTACK

HERO

Gravattack is a large, rocky alien who can control gravity. He's technically a small planet, and he has his own gravitational field so he can make objects orbit him at high speed before slinging them away long distances. He can also make nearby objects lighter or heavier, which means he can have fun throwing his opponents around, too.

HOME PLANET: Keplorr

SPECIES: Galilean

STRENGTHS: Can control gravity, and make objects orbit around him.

28

THE MORE THINGS CHANGE, PART 2

Down in Undertown, Ben couldn't believe what he was seeing – he'd had no idea this place even existed!

Ben and Rook chased the thugs through a maze of streets and into a train tunnel.Ben hit his Omnitrix, hoping for XLR8, but he got NRG.

Rook fired a restraint at the slowest thug to take him down. "Who's behind these alien shakedowns?" NRG demanded, leaning into the thug's face. But the thug's reply was drowned out by the frantic sounding of a horn – there was a train heading right for them!

Rook removed the restraint and threw the thug out of the way just in time. The train hit NRG and Rook with a nasty crunching sound. "You took out my brakes!" the driver yelled. They were on a collision course for the marketplace! NRG dug his feet into the rails and managed to stop the train before changing back into Ben. But the thug had disappeared.

Khyber and his dog had followed Ben and Rook down into Undertown, and found the marks NRG's feet had left on the track. "Hunt him up," Khyber rasped to his dog as it took off down the tunnel, following Ben's scent.

Ben stared at all the weird and wonderful things on sale in the market while Rook did some investigating. Rook caught up with Ben as he reached a stall selling fried tentacles on sticks.

Rook stepped in front of Ben, flashing his Plumber's badge at the stall owner.
"We're Plumbers working a case. Did you see a group of lowlifes run through here?"
The stall owner looked alarmed. "No! I don't know nothing, I don't see nothing!" He packed up his stall and drove off.

"Why'd you have to show your badge?" Ben sighed.

"This is my first time away from home," Rook began. "I may have misjudged—"

Rook stopped short as several nearby stalls went flying, and aliens began to scatter. Khyber's dog had transformed into a snarling alien beast and he was heading straight for Ben!

Ben hit the Omnitrix. Now would be a great time to go Humungousaur, but he got Waterhazard instead. Waterhazard launched himself at the beast. But the beast was strong – Waterhazard needed help.

Rook fired an electric bolo net at the beast's mouth, but it quickly broke free. "Two against one," Khyber whispered to himself as he watched. "The odds are becoming a bit … un-sporting." He whistled to his dog and it immediately returned to his side.

Waterhazard transformed back into Ben and made to set off after the beast, but he didn't know which way it had gone.

"Not to worry," Rook said. "My investigations earlier turned up a lead."

Rook led Ben to a social club for aliens who breathed cyano gas. He'd heard this was where they'd find Bubble Helmet. Ben peered through the foggy window – the gas would be poisonous to both of them.

"Hope you're OK waiting outside," Ben smirked. But Rook was already putting on an oxygen mask. Irritated, Ben hit the Omnitrix and transformed into Terraspin.

Rook kicked the door down. "Appendages in the air!" he demanded.

The aliens raised various arms, legs and tentacles.

Terraspin span round fast, sucking the gas out of the door so the aliens couldn't breathe. Loud coughs, gasps and wheezes filled the room, and they soon had a helpless Bubble Helmet cornered.

"Who's behind those shakedowns?" Terraspin demanded.

"I'll tell you, as soon as I can breathe!" Bubble Helmet gasped.

"That's a fair bargain," Rook said, handing his helmet over.

"Rook, no!" Terraspin shouted, but it was too late. Bubble Helmet fought his way loose and flew out of the door. Rook jumped on Terraspin's back and they set off after him.

"You've never dealt with actual bad guys before, have you?" Terraspin demanded.

"I've read about them in books and trained extensively," Rook said.

Bubble Helmet led them to the rest of the thugs who were gathered in a nearby alley, setting the controls on several Shakedown Machines just like the one they saw at Baumann's store.

The the Omnitrix timed out again – all Rook and Ben could do was hold up their hands in defeat as the thugs surrounded them.

Another figure emerged from the shadows – it was Psyphon. Ben couldn't believe it. Psyphon used to work for Vilgax!
"Get them, boys!" Psyphon spat gleefully.

Ben hit the Omnitrix and turned into Armodrillo as the thugs opened fire.

Psyphon fought Armodrillo one-on-one while Rook fought off the rest of the thugs. Psyphon hit Armodrillo with one of the Shakedown Machines, knocking him back out into the marketplace. He fired at one of Armodrillo's jackhammer arms, making it swell and jackhammer uncontrollably.

33

Armodrillo smashed into a stall and transformed back into Ben. Khyber's dog appeared out of nowhere, lunging straight for Ben. "Psyphon, call your dog off!" Ben gasped, straining out of the reach of the dog's massive jaws.

"He's not mine," Psyphon snarled, and fled. Ben transformed into Shocksquatch to take on the beast while Rook went after Psyphon.

Shocksquatch lured the beast into the train tunnel, and up a ladder encased in a metal tube. He sent a bolt of electricity through the tube, shocking the beast and knocking it out cold just as Rook arrived with Psyphon as his prisoner. The beast disappeared in a cloud of foul gas and retreated back to his master's ship before Ben and Rook could stop it. But all was not lost – they called Grandpa Max and handed Psyphon over to the Plumbers.

"You did well, old friend," Khyber soothed, when his dog returned to the ship. "This Ben Tennyson is more powerful than I imagined."

He surveyed the bones of the aliens he had killed, which decorated his ship. "He will be our greatest trophy. Khyber the Huntsman promises it."

THE END

SUPER SIDEKICK

Ben and Rook are on another mission to save the universe, and they need a sidekick! Think you're up to the job? Draw yourself in next to them.

WICKED WORDSEARCH

There are 20 alien names hidden in this wordsearch – can you spot them all? They could be hidden across, down, diagonally or even backwards!

A	L	I	E	N	X	B	A	L	L	W	E	E	V	I	L
H	C	G	S	R	A	T	H	E	P	O	N	O	T	G	B
E	U	A	K	D	I	W	F	C	V	L	K	L	Y	B	W
A	R	M	N	L	A	F	R	A	O	D	H	L	E	I	K
T	S	G	U	N	R	E	P	H	K	P	Y	I	K	G	W
B	W	E	G	N	O	O	H	M	R	Q	B	R	N	C	A
L	M	X	B	Q	G	N	O	D	A	T	E	D	O	H	H
A	S	Q	W	L	R	O	B	K	N	W	R	O	M	I	N
S	Z	F	S	L	G	Y	U	O	T	O	S	M	R	L	I
T	E	O	D	R	K	Z	I	S	L	A	M	R	E	L	K
O	A	U	B	L	O	X	X	E	A	T	G	A	D	O	C
T	I	R	Q	A	P	Y	J	E	S	U	E	Y	I	P	I
K	C	A	B	D	E	E	F	H	I	X	R	R	P	D	K
Q	G	R	A	V	A	T	T	A	C	K	Z	Y	S	S	O
W	O	M	T	H	C	T	A	U	Q	S	K	C	O	H	S
D	P	S	O	M	R	E	P	P	O	H	H	S	A	R	C

HIDDEN NAMES:

FEEDBACK
BLOXX
~~BALLWEEVIL~~
KICKIN HAWK
ROOK

SHOCKSQUATCH
GRAVATTACK
CRASHHOPPER
FOUR ARMS
~~HEATBLAST~~

ARMODRILLO
CANNONBOLT
DIAMONDHEAD
KHYBER
BIG CHILL

SPIDERMONKEY
~~HUMUNGOUSAUR~~
SWAMPFIRE
RATH
~~ALIEN X~~

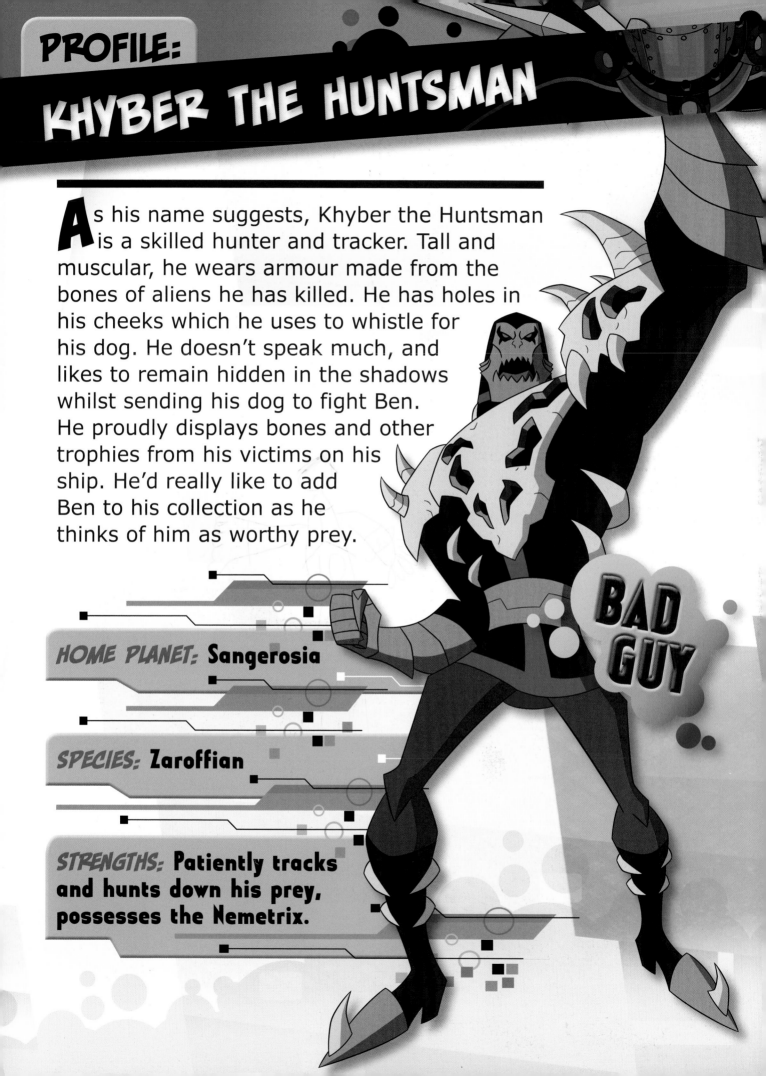

PROFILE:
KHYBER THE HUNTSMAN

As his name suggests, Khyber the Huntsman is a skilled hunter and tracker. Tall and muscular, he wears armour made from the bones of aliens he has killed. He has holes in his cheeks which he uses to whistle for his dog. He doesn't speak much, and likes to remain hidden in the shadows whilst sending his dog to fight Ben. He proudly displays bones and other trophies from his victims on his ship. He'd really like to add Ben to his collection as he thinks of him as worthy prey.

HOME PLANET: Sangerosia

SPECIES: Zaroffian

STRENGTHS: Patiently tracks and hunts down his prey, possesses the Nemetrix.

BAD GUY

Khyber's Nemetrix is the opposite of Ben's Omnitrix. It allows Khyber to turn his dog into the opposite of Ben's alien forms – the ten deadliest predators in the universe. When wearing the Nemetrix, Khyber's Dog has the power to defeat Ben in his alien forms.

KHYBER ATTACHES THE NEMETRIX TO HIS DOG'S COLLAR WHEN HE WANTS HIM TO TRANSFORM.

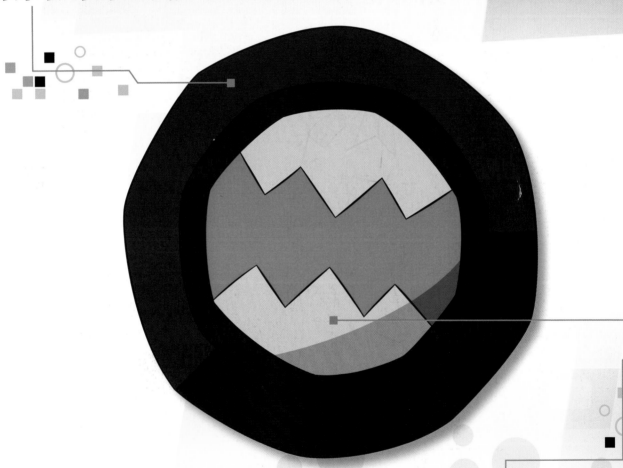

THE GREY PATTERN ON THE RED BACKGROUND LOOKS LIKE A MOUTH OF SHARP TEETH – VERY DIFFERENT FROM THE INTERGALACTIC PEACE-SYMBOL ON BEN'S OMNITRIX.

40

PROFILE:
KHYBER'S DOG

Khyber's dog is loyal to his master and never leaves Khyber's side unless under orders to attack. By attaching the Nemetrix to the dog's collar, Khyber can turn him into ten different predators so he can fight Ben in alien form. Here are the predators Ben's had to deal with so far:

CRABDOZER (Heatblast's predator species)
Impervious to fire, this predator looks like a jurassic rhino and is just as strong.

BUGLIZARD (Stinkfly's predator species)
This lizard predator has four eyes and massive jaws filled with sharp teeth.

SLAMWORM (Armodrillo's predator species)
Slamworm looks like an enormous worm with spikes and sharp teeth.

MUCILLATOR (Crashhopper's predator species)
This predator looks like a grotesque human figure, and uses a sticky substance to trap his opponents. Yuck!

VICIOUS VILLAINS

BAD GUYS

Of course, there are plenty of other bad guys for Ben and Rook to deal with aside from Khyber and his dog. They might not be quite so dangerous or intelligent, but they're still a real pain!

PSYPHON

Psyphon used to be alien overlord Vilgax's right hand man. But since Vilgax's defeat, he's toughened up and put himself in charge of Undertown's alien thugs. His mission is to become the most feared alien in Undertown and he's been sending his thugs out to threaten peace-loving aliens.

SPECIES: Unknown
HOME PLANET: Unknown
STRENGTHS: Super strength. Possesses alien tech which he uses to protect himself.

MALWARE

Malware is a highly dangerous Galvanic Mechamorph. Something went wrong when he was created, leaving him a mutant. He eventually managed to cure himself, becoming even more vicious and deadly in the process. Malware desperately wants to take the Omnitrix from Ben, but hasn't managed it yet.

SPECIES: Galvanic Mechamorph
HOME PLANET: Galvan B
STRENGTHS: Very intelligent, can absorb any technology he touches, sharp claws.

FISTRICK

Fistrick is a human thug who thinks of himself as a businessman. He steals alien tech then sells it on to the highest bidder. He hangs out in an abandoned warehouse with his thugs and spends a lot of time working out.

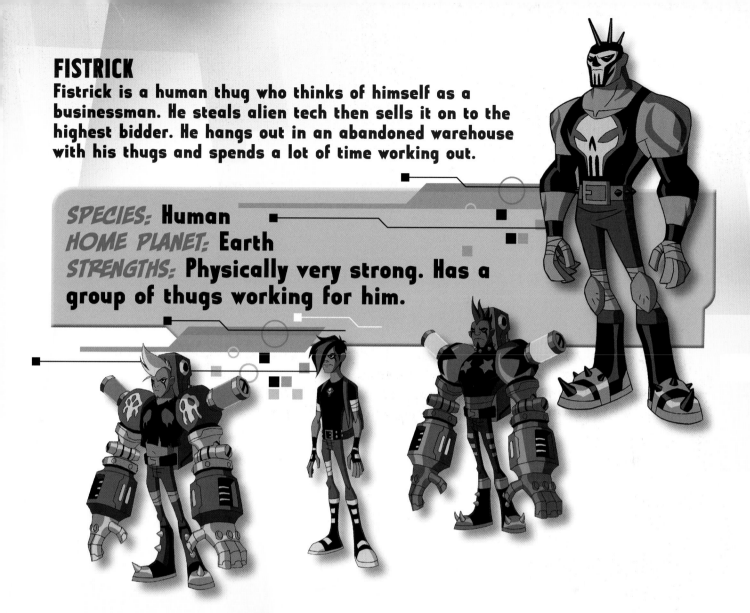

SPECIES: Human
HOME PLANET: Earth
STRENGTHS: Physically very strong. Has a group of thugs working for him.

The Undertown Thugs

The Undertown thugs are a group of aliens led by Psyphon who go around terrorising other aliens and stealing Taydenite from them. Liam, Bubblehead and Fistina are the leaders.

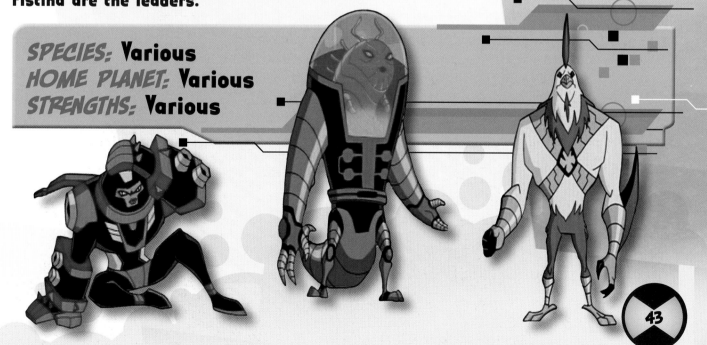

SPECIES: Various
HOME PLANET: Various
STRENGTHS: Various

UNSCRAMBLE

Rook has sent Ben a coded message. Can you unscramble each word to reveal the secret?

1 A	2 B	3 C	4 D	5 E	6 F	7 G	8 H	9 I
10 J	11 K	12 L	13 M	14 N	15 O	16 P	17 Q	18 R
19 S	20 T	21 U	22 V	23 W	24 X	25 Y	26 Z

13 5 5 20

2 1 3 11

1 20

20 8 5

19 8 9 16

Write your answer here.

___ ___ ___ ___ ___ ___ ___ ___ ___ ___ ___ ___

___ ___ ___ ___ ___ ___ ___ ___ ___ ___ ___ ___

A JOLT FROM THE PAST

SIX YEARS AGO IN BELLWOOD ...

Ten-year-old Ben Tennyson had a situation on his hands. A Megawhatt was wreaking havoc in his local smoothie bar, Mr Smoothy, and it was up to him to deal with the problem. Ben transformed into Stinkfly and fired several shots of goo at the Megawhatt, but they didn't hold it for long. The Megawhatt transformed into a bolt of electricity and shot into the nearest smoothie machine where it fired a stream of smoothie at Stinkfly, causing the Omnitrix to time out. Ben chased the Megawhatt out onto the street where it headed for the nearest overhead power cable and began to multiply. Soon the sky was filled with cackling Megawhatts.

Fortunately Ben had one alien hero at his disposal who could handle electricity. He transformed into Feedback and zapped the energy from the Megawhatts. Without energy, they immediately fell asleep, drifting gently back to the ground. Ben sincerely hoped that was the last he'd see of these guys ...

PRESENT DAY ...

Sixteen-year-old Ben Tennyson wandered into the Plumbers' secret underground base, slurping a smoothie. "Sorry I'm late," he said lazily to Grandpa Max and Rook.

"You're not on your own schedule any more, Ben. You can't keep your partner waiting," Grandpa Max scolded.

Ben sighed. "Come on, Rook, I'm parked over here."

"We'll take mine," Rook replied, gesturing towards a nearby delivery truck.

Ben wasn't impressed with Rook's ride, but Rook took out his keys and hit the alarm button, and the truck transformed into a high tech, heavily armed hover vehicle. "Sometimes, you're actually kinda awesome," Ben admitted.

As they set off to patrol Bellwood, Ben began to apologize.

"I'm sorry I left you waiting. I just don't want to change how I work. I've saved the universe a million times, at least!"

Rook nodded. "That is why I look forward to this. I hope the real Ben Tennyson lives up to the legends."

Ben perked up. "There are legends?"

"They can't all be true, though. Alien X is just a rumour that a fan made up and put on the extranet, right?"

"Alien X is real," Ben assured him.

"Show me. Change into Alien X right now!"

"I better not. It's a whole … thing."

"Just as I thought." Rook looked disappointed.

"Find us a little heroing to do, and you can tell me if I live up to the legend," Ben said confidently.

They spotted a teenage guy crossing the road, talking on a phone that was clearly made from alien tech. They parked the truck and began to follow him. But they weren't stealthy enough – the teenager suddenly span round, blasting a powerful beam of energy at them from his phone. He sprinted to a car parked nearby and drove off.

Ben hit his Omnitrix, crossing his fingers for Big Chill, but transformed into Heatblast. Heatblast took to the sky to follow the car, with Rook right behind him in his ship. Heatblast melted one of the car's tyres with a firebolt, and the vehicle skidded to a stop in the middle of the street.

Heatblast landed, transforming back into Ben. Rook grabbed the guy as he tried to make a run for it.

"What is your deal?" the guy demanded. "I wasn't doing anything!"

"Alien communicator, alien weapon … please tell me you work for someone big and dangerous so I can kick his butt!" Ben grinned. The guy's car was making odd noises, so Rook lifted the bonnet. A yellow energy cylinder inside exploded and a bolt of electricity shot out into the street, hitting a puddle and creating a sizzling cloud of steam. When the steam cleared, Ben and Rook could see a Megawhatt standing there.

The Megawatt made a run for the nearest electricity source – an overhead power cable – and duplicated itself. Ben was worried – he'd dealt with Megawatts before and he knew how quickly they could multiply.

The Megawhatts took off down an electricity cable, sending sparks flying behind them and cutting the power to the traffic lights on the streets below. Ben and Rook had no choice but to follow them, leaving the teenage guy free to escape. Ben transformed into Clockwork. Heavy Clockwork couldn't move very fast, but he still managed to keep up with the Megawhatts – they kept stopping and looking back, almost as if they wanted him to follow them.

After several blocks the Megawhatts shot inside a warehouse. Clockwork transformed back into Ben, and he and Rook headed in after them. An enormous containment tank stood in the middle of the warehouse. Dozens of Megawhatts were trapped inside individual pods and the two free Megawhatts were banging desperately on the glass, trying to free them. "I see it, but I don't believe it," Ben whispered. "The Megawhatts need our help!"

"Someone has set up a factory that uses them as a power source!" Rook was disgusted. They ducked behind a wall as a thuggish human figure appeared on an overhead walkway.

"Hey, two of the batteries got out!" he shouted. Two more thugs appeared on ground level. They fired high tech weapons at the Megawhatts, immobilizing them in an energy field then sucking the Megawhatts into the weapons. Another thug sneaked up on Ben and Rook and zapped them with an energy field. They were helpless.

The factory doors slid open and a mean-looking guy appeared, flanked by the guy they'd been chasing.

"Looks like spies, Fistrick," one of the thugs addressed the mean-looking guy.

"Spies, in my house of business?" Fistrick snarled.

"You steal alien tech, and then use alien hostages to charge it!" Ben accused.

Fistrick sneered at Ben. "I mass produce it, and sell it to the highest bidder. It's just good business, bro."

Rook activated a small device. "What is that?" Fistrick demanded.

"An electronic entanglement disrupter," Rook smiled, as the energy surrounding them flickered and faded.

Ben hit the Omnitrix and transformed into Bloxx, destroying the floor of the warehouse with his giant fists. Rook took care of the nearest thug with his Proto-tool.

"You just made a big mistake, bro," Fistrick growled as Ben transformed back.

Fistrick and his thugs disappeared down a trapdoor in the floor. Fistrick emerged a moment later, wearing an enormous suit of alien armour. Ben and Rook backed away – how were they going to take him down now?

"You never asked why we needed so many Megawhatts," Fistrick sneered. He turned around, and they saw the Megawhatts were attached to the back of the suit.

"A Class Twelve armoured mecha suit!" Rook gasped.

Fistrick fired his weapons and several laser-guided rockets came flying towards them. The explosions threw them across the room and they landed hard. Rook jumped up and fired at Fistrick.

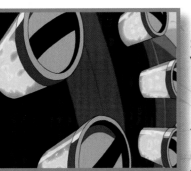

"Stop shooting!" Ben shouted. "You might hit the Megawhatts!"

Ben hit the Omnitrix and transformed into an enormous rocky alien he'd never seen before – Gravattack!

Fistrick knocked Gravattack outside, through the warehouse wall. But Gravattack fought back, and to his delight he found he could control gravity! He forced Fistrick backwards, then lifted him high into the air before slamming him into the ground. Rook jumped on Fistrick's back to free the Megawhatts. But Fistrick fired a shot at Rook, sending him sprawling across the parking lot. With Rook out of action Fistrick pinned Gravattack to the ground and hit him with his massive hands.

A crane hook came flying out of nowhere, sending Fistrick flying into the factory roof. Gravattack looked around, and saw Rook smiling from the crane's cabin.

"I think I can separate the Megawhatts from the suit!" Rook shouted, drawing his Proto-Tool. "But it will be a difficult shot. Try to get the suit to stop moving." Gravattack lifted Fistrick into the air again before slamming him back down into the ground.

"You might be able to withstand forty Gs, but I don't think the docks can," Gravattack smirked, pushing down on Fistrick until the docks crumbled beneath him and collapsed into the water.

Gravattack had some fun dunking Fistrick in and out of the water. Then Rook took aim with his bow and hit the back of Fistrick's suit. The Megawhatts popped out of their canisters and scuttled away, cackling with glee.

Fistrick had just enough energy left to haul himself back onto the dock and launch his remaining rockets at Gravattack. Gravattack turned himself into a ball of rock and pulled the rockets and Fistrick into his orbit. He slung Fistrick up into the air and sent the rockets after him. They hit their target, exploding loudly and destroying Fistrick's suit.

Ben transformed back.
"That was not easy," Rook gasped.
"It never is," Ben smiled.

Grandpa Max arrived with Plumber backup and took Fistrick and his thugs away. "I hear there's a colony of Megawhatts that helps power Undertown," Grandpa Max said, pointing to a canister of Megawhatts who were being taken away by Plumbers. The Megawhatts smiled and waved at Ben. Ben waved back. "Any time, guys!"

THE END

50

COLOUR THE BLOXX

Bloxx can shapeshift into different forms. Give him some colour and bring him to life!

ALIEN DESIGNER

If you had the Omnitrix, what kind of alien would you turn into? Create your very own alien in the space below. You might want to use the pictures of the Omnitrix aliens for inspiration, or you could try something completely different – it's up to you!

Kickin' Hawk looks like a large, alien rooster. He has sharp claws and two large talons coming out of his arms, which make him a very tough fighter. And you don't want to be on the receiving end of one of his powerful kicks!

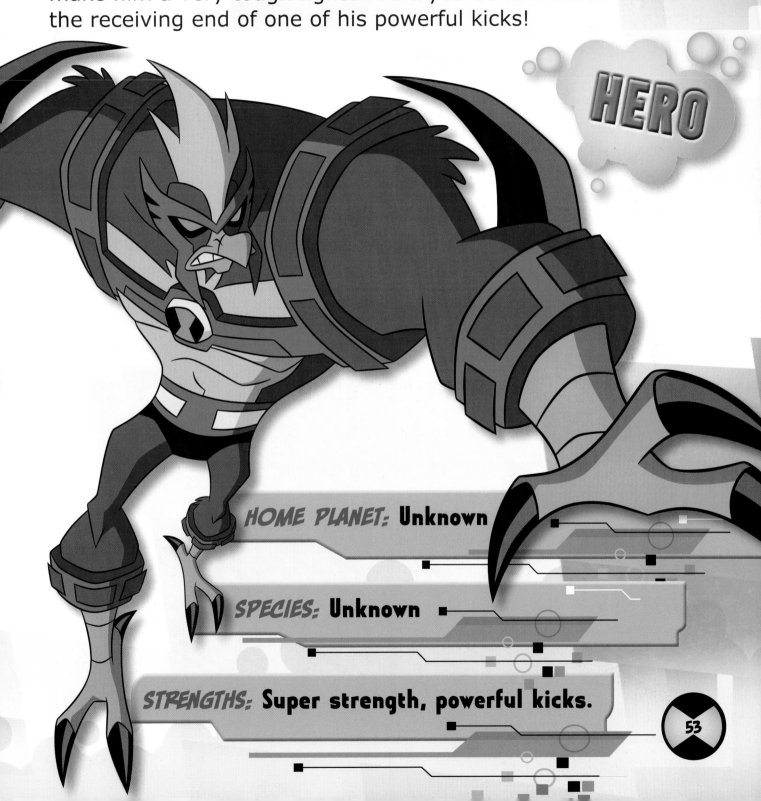

HERO

HOME PLANET: Unknown

SPECIES: Unknown

STRENGTHS: Super strength, powerful kicks.

53

BALLWEEVIL

HERO

Ballweevil is a tiny, insect-like alien who uses balls of spit to destroy things. He spits out a small gummy ball, jumps on top of it and rolls it over debris to collect it. The ball gets bigger and bigger until it's large enough to fire at his opponents. It will explode on contact, and the bigger the ball, the bigger the boom!

HOME PLANET: Unknown

SPECIES: Unknown

STRENGTHS: Can spit out sticky balls which he can fire at his enemies, make explode or absorb things with.

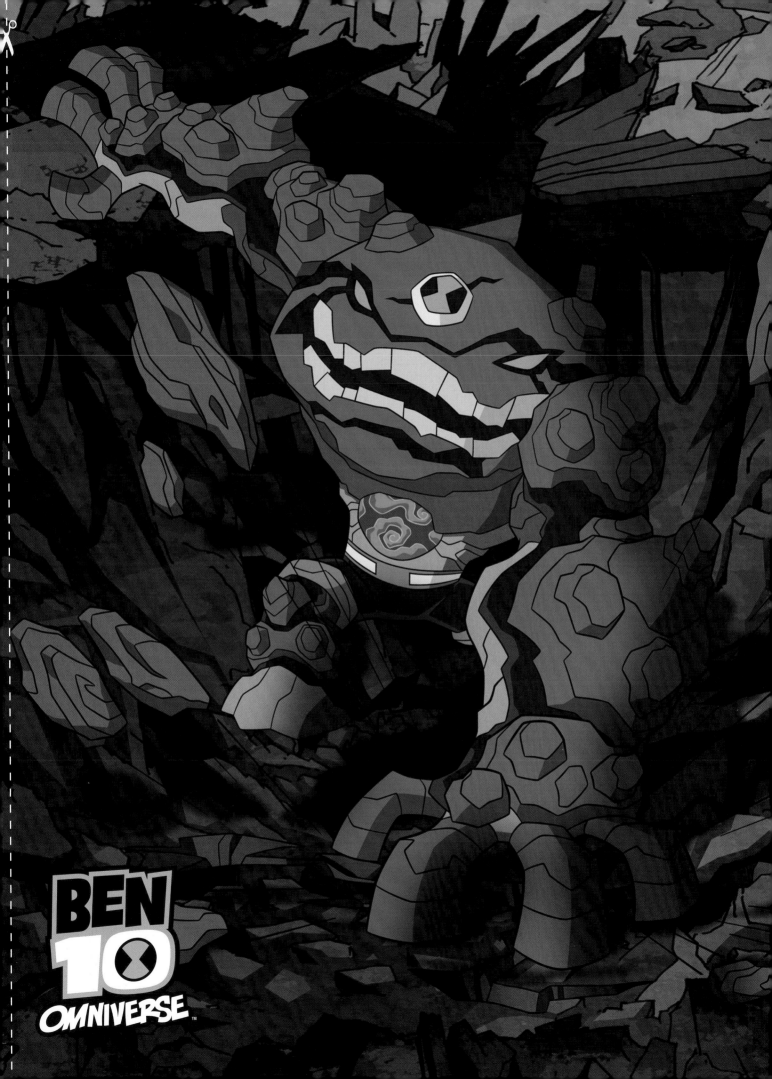

RACE BACK TO BASE

Ben and Rook have made an amazing discovery down in Undertown. Now they need to report back to Grandpa Max at the Plumbers' Base, pronto. But the streets of Undertown can be very confusing. Can you help them find the quickest way back to Rook's ship through the maze?

START

FINISH

TROUBLE HELIX

Khyber the Huntsman was on a late night recon mission. He'd bypassed the security systems at the Plumbers' secret base and snuck into the records room. Quietly, he loaded a video record and a 3-D hologram of the planet Galvan Prime appeared on the screen.

Six Years Earlier, on Galvan Prime ...

Azmuth, a Galvan scientist, was hard at work in his laboratory with his assistant Albedo when the door suddenly burst open. Grandpa Max fell into the room with several Galvans attempting to drag him back out.

"Azmuth! I can't take it any more. You've got to do something about Ben!" Grandpa Max pleaded. Azmuth didn't even look up from his work. "As you can see, I'm exceedingly busy."

XLR8, zipped into the lab. Ben's eleven-year-old cousin Gwen came bursting in after him, puffing and panting. XLR8 ran around the lab at high speed, picking up random objects and asking a constant stream of questions.

"THIS is what I've been dealing with," Grandpa Max explained. "The Omnitrix is malfunctioning. Ben's been trapped as a different alien every week!"

"Not my concern," Azmuth insisted.

XLR8 was playing with one of Azmuth's experiments. There was a small explosion and a puff of smoke. "Hey!"' Azmuth yelled. He jumped on XLR8, tapped a sequence on the Omnitrix symbol on his chest and XLR8 transformed back into ten-year-old Ben.

Grandpa Max told Gwen to watch Ben while he had a private word with Azmuth. Ben looked sulkily out of the window, watching what looked like a shooting star fly across the sky.

The shooting star Ben had seen was actually a massive meteorite. It crash-landed in a swamp outside the city, and a black and yellow alien form emerged.

A Galvan security officer immediately rushed over. "Galvanic Mechamorph Subspecies! You are forbidden from entering the city. You're to stay on Galvan B—" the officer began, but the Mechamorph reached out and crushed him in his hand, dropped him into the swamp then shot up into the sky.

The Mechamorph headed into the centre of the city, roaring with rage and destroying everything it passed.

Back inside Azmuth's lab, Ben watched the path of explosions down in the city coming closer and closer. He couldn't stand it any more – he hit the Omnitrix, transforming into Feedback, and shot out of the lab before Gwen could stop him.

Feedback quickly tracked down the Mechamorph and zapped him with a bolt of electricity.

"The Omnitrix! I want it!" the Mechamorph cried, lunging at Feedback. As they wrestled, Feedback was thrown backwards and transformed back into Ben. Ben quickly hit the Omnitrix again and changed into Four Arms.

Four Arms swung the Mechamorph round and round, then sent it flying into the air. Unfortunately it crashed straight through one of Azmuth's lab windows.

Four Arms raced to the lab, changed back into Ben and found the Mechamorph standing face to face with Azmuth.
"Malware, this is not the way," Azmuth said.

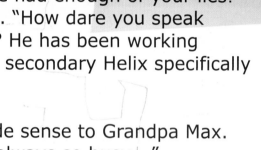

"You promised me an upgrade! You said you'd make me like the others!" Malware screamed.
"Your condition is complex. It has taken more time than I anticipated to—"
"No more time! I've had enough of your lies!"
Albedo was furious. "How dare you speak to Azmuth that way? He has been working tirelessly to create a secondary Helix specifically to treat you!"

Suddenly it all made sense to Grandpa Max. "That's what you're always so busy ..."
Azmuth nodded. "The second Helix is not finished. To use it now could cause untold

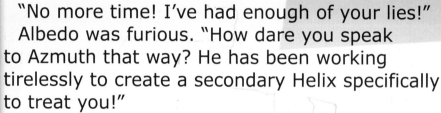

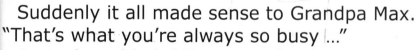

destruction. I need more time to help you."
But Malware wouldn't listen. He grabbed Albedo, absorbed the second Helix into his chest and blasted off into the sky heading straight for the moon, Galvan B. They all followed Malware outside and stared up at the moon. Grandpa Max ordered Ben and Azmuth to get into his Plumber Ship. Gwen went back into the lab to await instructions while the ship took off for the moon.
On the way, Azmuth explained the history of the Galvanic Mechamorphs and how Malware came into being.

"Galvan B was once much like Earth's moon: miles of dead rock, no atmosphere, no day or night. It was the perfect environment to conduct a planet-wide experiment. I wanted to make Galvan B a place upon which life would thrive."

Azmuth remembered the Helix radiating energy outwards and a metallic-looking fungus springing up all over the surface of Galvan B.

"The results were beyond anything I could have hoped for. Not only was Galvan B inhabitable, but my experiment had created a brand new technorganic species – the Galvanic Mechamorphs."

Azmuth told them how the Galvans had given the moon to the Galvanic Mechamorphs rather than trying to rule them. The Mechamorphs became their peaceful new neighbours.

Azmuth remembered the day he had shut down the Helix for good. The Helix had released one last surge of energy. This incomplete surge had created a corrupted Mechamorph – Malware.

"Unlike all the others of his kind, Malware had the ability to not just mimic tech, it became him. But at a terrible price," Azmuth told them. Malware couldn't touch anything without absorbing its power, including other Mechamorphs.

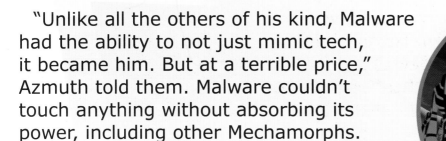

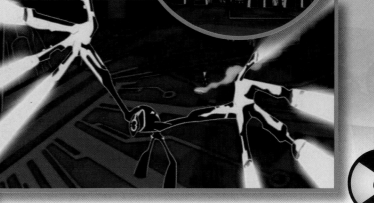

"I've tried many times to help him, but his condition is complex. I believe he is going to link the old Helix with the new one, to try to rewrite his life code."

They landed on Galvan B. Azmuth stopped to help some half-dead Mechamorphs that Malware had drained of energy, so Ben and Grandpa Max set off to deal with Malware alone. Before Grandpa Max could think of a plan, Ben transformed into Heatblast and ran on ahead to find Malware. He found Malware at the original Helix, ordering Albedo to complete his upgrade.

"Do not interfere!" Malware roared, knocking Heatblast off his feet and raising his huge hand to drain him.

Grandpa Max arrived just in time – he hit Malware with a laser stream from a blaster gun. Leaving Heatblast to deal with Malware, he ran over to Albedo who was still working on the Helix.
"Stop fiddling with that thing. We're getting out. Now."
"It's too late! If I don't complete the link with the primary Helix, the secondary Helix will cycle out of control and destroy the moon, with us on it!"

Albedo pressed one final button and the second Helix powered into life. Malware whirled round at the sound. "At last! I will be cured!" he cried, running forwards and grabbing two glowing rods attached to the Helix.

Heatblast tried to stop him but was knocked backwards with the force of the power surging through Malware, and changed back into Ben. Malware's yellow energy lines were turning orange. He began to grow taller and more powerful. Albedo had

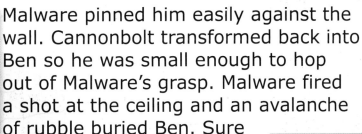

deliberately rigged the second Helix to overload and destroy Malware, but instead, Malware was transformed into a Mechamorph even more powerful than the others.

"Upgrade complete," Malware smiled. Ben transformed into Cannonbolt but Malware pinned him easily against the wall. Cannonbolt transformed back into Ben so he was small enough to hop out of Malware's grasp. Malware fired a shot at the ceiling and an avalanche of rubble buried Ben. Sure the Omnitrix was within his grasp, Malware began

to dig, but Diamondhead emerged from the rubble, firing crystal shards at Malware! Soon he was completely covered and unable to move.

"That's right! You can't get through crystal, can you?" Diamondhead laughed. The battle was over.

Khyber paused the record and the image froze.

"This has been ... illuminating," he whispered to himself. He copied the files to a device in his pocket, and silently left the building. Outside, Khyber patted his dog and smiled.

"We have everything we need now, boy. No secrets are safe."

THE END

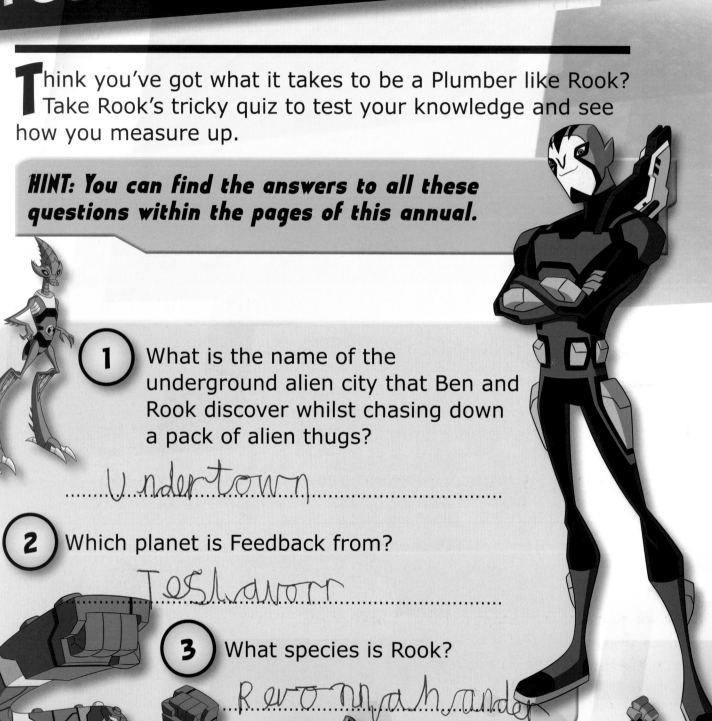

ROOK'S QUIZ

Think you've got what it takes to be a Plumber like Rook? Take Rook's tricky quiz to test your knowledge and see how you measure up.

HINT: You can find the answers to all these questions within the pages of this annual.

1 What is the name of the underground alien city that Ben and Rook discover whilst chasing down a pack of alien thugs?

Undertown

2 Which planet is Feedback from?

Teslavorr

3 What species is Rook?

Revonnahander

4 Which Omnitrix alien does Ben transform into when chasing alien thugs through Undertown's train tunnel in The More Things Change, Part 2?

....

5 How old is Gwen in the story Trouble Helix?

....

6 Which alien does ten-year-old Ben turn into at the beginning of Trouble Helix?

....

7 Which alien does Ben turn into to defeat Malware at the end of Trouble Helix?

....

8 Which predator does Khyber's Dog become to fight Crashhopper?

....

Check your answers on page 66 and add up your score. Then check your total against the categories below to see whether you made the cut!

7–8 correct answers: Congratulations – your alien knowledge is impressive and you'd make a fine Plumber!

4–6 correct answers: Good, but more experience and training needed if you want to help Ben save the universe. You're not quite ready.

1–3 correct answers: You need to enrol at the Plumber's Academy immediately. Serious training needed before you can become a Plumber!

ANSWERS

PAGE 18
ODD OMNITRIX OUT

Omnitrix 'E' is the correct one.

PAGE 19
UNDERTOWN SHOWDOWN

PAGE 24-25
LOOK AGAIN

PAGE 26
ALIEN SWARM

There are 14 aliens.

PAGE 38
WICKED WORDSEARCH

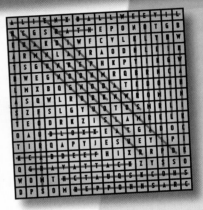

PAGE 44
UNSCRAMBLE

The message reads: MEET BACK AT THE SHIP

PAGE 57
RACE BACK TO BASE

PAGE 64
ROOK'S QUIZ

1. Undertown
2. Teslavorr
3. Revonnahgander
4. NRG
5. Eleven
6. XLR8
7. Diamondhead
8. Mucillator

66

READER SURVEY

Ask a grown-up to help you fill in this form and post it to the address at the end by 28th February 2014, or you can fill in the survey online at **www.egmont.co.uk/ben10survey2014**

ONE LUCKY READER WILL WIN £150 OF BOOK TOKENS! FIVE RUNNERS-UP WILL WIN A £25 BOOK TOKEN EACH.

NATIONAL BOOK tokens

1. WHO BOUGHT THIS BEN 10 ANNUAL?

- ◯ Me
- ☑ Parent/guardian
- ◯ Grandparent
- ◯ Other (please specify)

_____

2. WHY DID THEY BUY IT?

- ◯ Christmas present
- ◯ Birthday present
- ☑ I'm a collector
- ◯ Other (please specify)

_____

3. WHAT ARE YOUR FAVOURITE PARTS OF THE BEN 10 ANNUAL?

Stories	☑ Really like	◯ Like	◯ Don't like
Puzzles	☑ Really like	◯ Like	◯ Don't like
Quizzes	☑ Really like	◯ Like	◯ Don't like
Colouring	☑ Really like	◯ Like	◯ Don't like
Character Profiles	☑ Really like	◯ Like	◯ Don't like

4. DO YOU THINK THE STORIES ARE TOO LONG, TOO SHORT OR ABOUT RIGHT?

- ◯ Too long
- ◯ Too short
- ☑ About right

5. DO YOU THINK THE ACTIVITIES ARE TOO HARD, TOO EASY OR ABOUT RIGHT?

- ◯ Too hard
- ◯ Too easy
- ☑ About right

6. APART FROM BEN, WHO ARE YOUR FAVOURITE CHARACTERS?

(1) ROOK

(2) Fistrick

(3) Kevin

67

7. WHICH OTHER ANNUALS DO YOU LIKE?

(1) D mniverse

(2) ulrimate alien

(3) Ben 10

8. WHAT IS YOUR FAVOURITE ...

(1) ... app or website?

Ben 10 Make your own game

(2) ... console game?

Skylanders Swap Force

(3) ... magazine?

Ben 10

(4) ... book?

~~Dieary~~ Diary of a Wimpy kid

9. WHAT ARE YOUR FAVOURITE TV PROGRAMMES?

(1) Regular show

(2) Ben 10

(3) A dventure time

10. WOULD YOU LIKE TO GET THE BEN 10 ANNUAL AGAIN NEXT YEAR?

☑ Yes   ○ No

Why? Because ~~it~~ it is great

THANK YOU!

(Please ask your parent/guardian to complete)

Child's name: _____ Age: 7 (Boy)/ Girl

Parent/guardian name: _____

Parent/guardian signature: _____

Parent/guardian email address: _____

Daytime telephone number: _____

Please cut out and post to:
BEN 10 Reader Survey
Egmont UK Limited
The Yellow Building
1 Nicholas Road
London W11 4AN

GOOD LUCK!

○ **Please send me the Egmont Monthly Catch-Up Newsletter.**